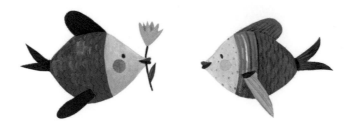

The artwork in this book was created using watercolour
and acrylic paints, as well as digital methods.

Translated by Polly Lawson. First published in German as *Mina entdeckt eine neue Welt* by Carlsen Verlag GmbH, Hamburg in 2020. First published in English by Floris Books, Edinburgh in 2022 First published in the USA in 2023. Text and illustrations © 2020 Carlsen Verlag GmbH English version © 2022 Floris Books. All rights reserved. No part of this book may be reproduced without the prior permission of Floris Books, Edinburgh www.florisbooks.co.uk British Library CIP data available ISBN 978-178250-811-3 Printed in China by Leo Paper Products Ltd

Floris Books supports sustainable forest management by printing this book on materials made from wood that comes from responsible sources and reclaimed material

Mina Belongs Here

Written by
Sandra Niebuhr-Siebert

Illustrated by
Lars Baus

Floris
Books

It was the night before Mina's first day at her new kindergarten. She didn't want to go, but her mama said she would have fun there and people would be kind.

Mina tossed and turned in bed, and dreamed about lots of strange things.

In the morning, Mama took her to kindergarten. Mina heard children laughing and playing behind the door. She stood on her tiptoes and peeked through the keyhole…

Hello, Mina, come in!

Mina said goodbye to Mama and shuffled shyly inside. The room was very noisy and very busy. Mina spotted a lonely teddy bear. She wondered if he would like a hug.

A woman with friendly eyes
spoke to her. The words sounded like
"HelowMinacummin", but Mina only
understood her own name.

She didn't know how to reply, so
she stayed quiet.

When Mama came to take her home, Mina nestled into her long, silky skirt… And then, in her own language, she started to talk. She talked and talked and talked.

Mina told Mama about her kind teacher, and how soft Teddy's fur was, and a girl with a sprinkle of freckles and long red braids who wanted to play, and everything she could remember about her day.

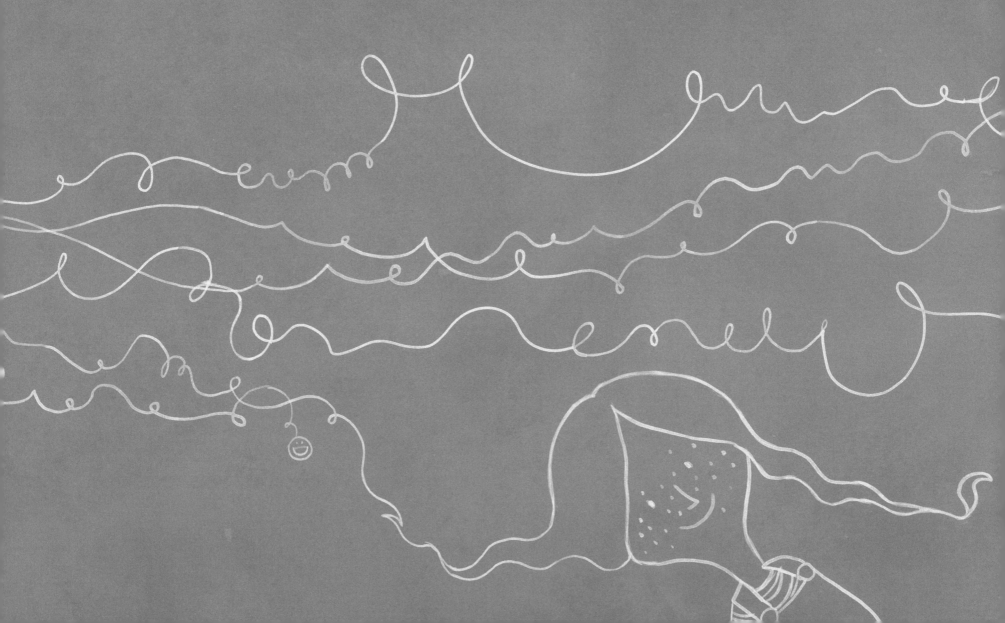

That night, Mina dreamed...

A few days later, Mina was playing
with her new friend Ava. They didn't
understand each other's words, but
together they looked after Teddy,
who had a stomach ache.

While the children played, their
teacher made some special cards.

At bedtime, Mina told Mama about her new best friend Ava, and her clever teacher who showed her picture cards, and how sorry she felt for kindergarten Teddy with the stomach ache, until her tongue got tired and her eyes felt heavy.

That night, Mina dreamed…

Mina soon started to enjoy eating lunch with her new friends. One day they were having yummy spaghetti, and she really wanted some more.

When her teacher Ms Flutter asked a question, Mina beamed and said, "Yes!" But Ms Flutter just smiled, nodded and moved on.

What did she say wrong? Mina knew more words now, but she still got confused.

After lunch, they listened to a story about Baba Yaga, a famous fairy-tale witch. Mina didn't understand all of the story, but she liked the way the witch's name rhymed: *Baba Yaga*. It made her think of bubbling potions!

She imagined the wicked witch in the story and practised saying her name. She whispered the sounds and stretched them – *Baah-baah Yaah-gaah*. She sang them and rolled her tongue – *Bar-bar Yar-gar*. It sounded wonderfully mysterious.

At home, Mina practised saying all the words and sounds she was learning.
When she said the word 'squirrel', her tongue tumbled and turned like a somersault and tickled her mouth!

That night, Mina dreamed…

Mina used her new words more and more. Before long, she could talk to all her friends and understand most of Ms Flutter's questions, even if she had to think for a moment. Teddy was feeling better too, and he liked to join in their games.

"Mina, come and listen to this!" Ms Flutter called.

Ms Flutter was playing a song in Mina's language!
Mina started to sing along excitedly. Her friends didn't
understand the words, but they still enjoyed listening
with her.

"Maybe one day they'll learn some of my words,
like I learned theirs," Mina thought, and smiled.

Later, while her friends were running around outside,
Mina drew a surprise for them on the picture wall. She
wanted to share how she was feeling and make the
classroom even more beautiful.

Picture Wall.

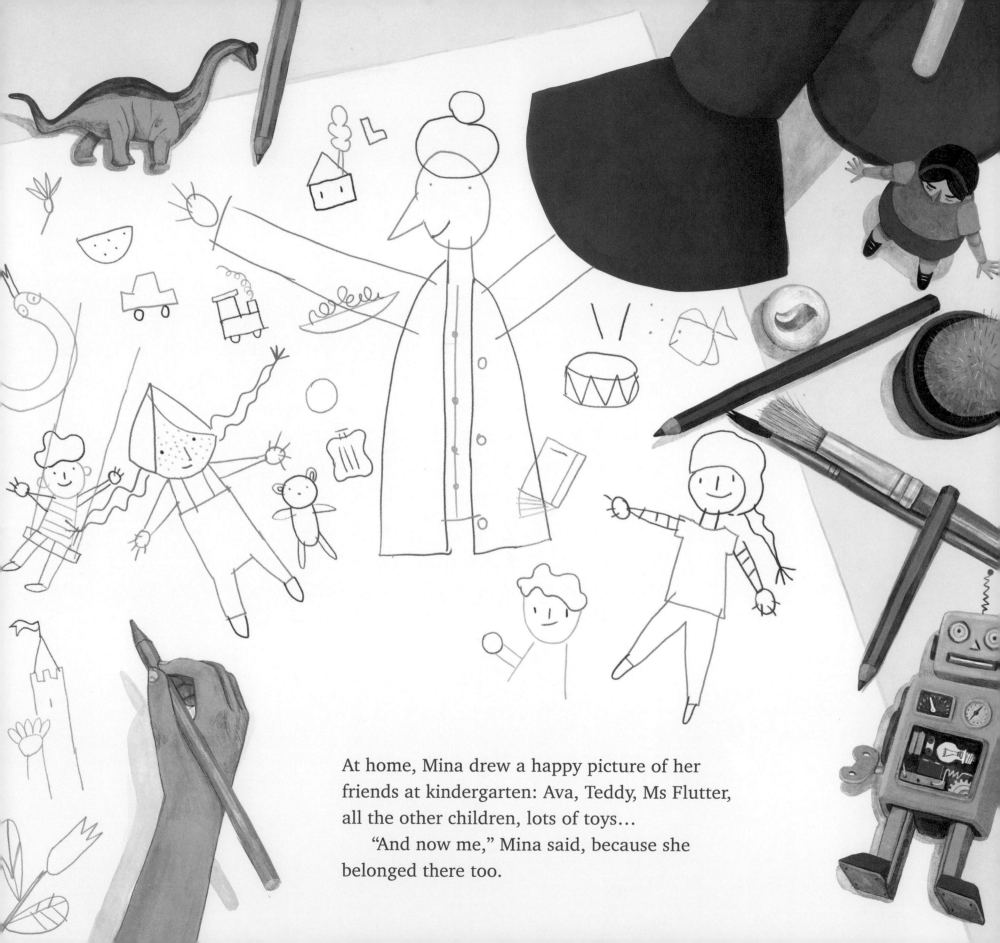

At home, Mina drew a happy picture of her friends at kindergarten: Ava, Teddy, Ms Flutter, all the other children, lots of toys…

"And now me," Mina said, because she belonged there too.

That night, Mina dreamed…

One day, the kindergarten door opened and a new boy shuffled shyly inside.

"Hello, Tarek, come in!" called Ms Flutter.

The boy looked around, but he didn't reply.

Mina walked over and gave him Teddy to cuddle. "I'm Mina," she said, patting her chest. "Come and play."

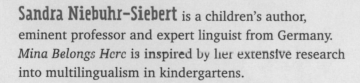

Sandra Niebuhr–Siebert is a children's author, eminent professor and expert linguist from Germany. *Mina Belongs Here* is inspired by her extensive research into multilingualism in kindergartens.

Sandra is also honorary head of the reading jury for the KIMI seal programme for diversity in children's books. She is happiest working in her kitchen at home in Potsdam, Germany, where she lives with her two daughters, their dog, rabbits and guinea pigs.

Lars Baus is an illustrator from Bavaria, Germany. He studied illustration and animation at the Münster Academy of Art, working briefly as a graphic designer before becoming a full-time freelance illustrator.

Lars has illustrated several children's books, and worked on commissions for children's museums and nature conservation associations. He loves to draw in his shared studio, where he enjoys the light and treats from a nearby bakery. Lars lives with his family in Münster, Germany.